THE BOY
AND
THE BOX

Leila Boukarim & Shameer Bismilla
Illustrated by Barbara Moxham

mc Marshall Cavendish
Children

For Luca, Alex, Haig, Pop, Kimi, Missak, Charles, Giorgio,
Alex Sr., Matteo, and all the big-hearted boys and men in my life —
past and present — whom I love and admire. You make this world better.
– L.B.

To my students from Grade E-2A (2019/2020) at the German European School
Singapore. Thank you for all the wonderful stories you've shared. To all the
boys in my classes. Be forgiving, fascinated and fearless. But most importantly,
be you!
– S.B.

For Markus, Kai, Tom, Sam and all boys brave enough to be true to themselves.
– B.M.

The boy came into the world small,
but full of wonder.

He gazed at the path before him

and his heart raced with excitement.

The boy sauntered along, enjoying every little step.

He came to a plain empty box...

...and imagined all the things he could do with it.

"Is that a box?"
a girl asked.

"It's anything I want it to be,"
the boy said.

"That's wonderful,"
she said and waved goodbye.

The boy's legs grew longer and stronger.

They were excellent for running
and skipping and walking backwards.

The boy sidestepped and looped around
and even rolled if he felt like it.

It wasn't long, however, before the path he was on…

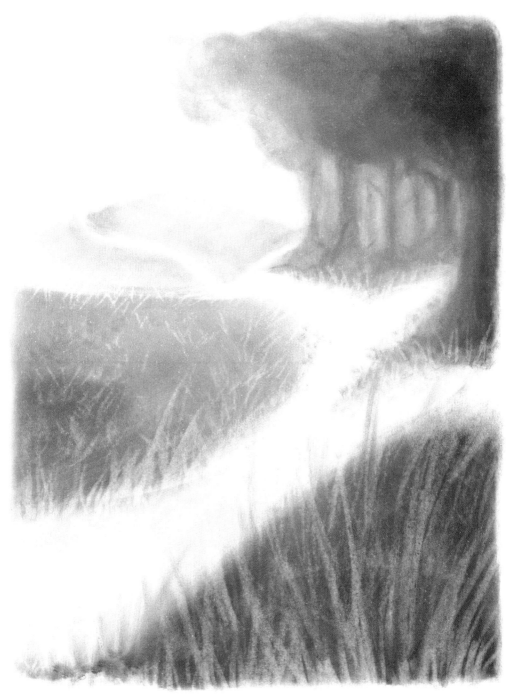

...split.

The boy crinkled his nose, squinted,

and stepped onto the path he felt was right.

But someone had something to say
about that.

"You really shouldn't go that way."

"Why not?"
said the boy.

"Because *this* is the path for you.
It will make you tough,"
the person said.

"But I have a strong feeling about this one," the boy said.

"Boys don't use their feelings to make important decisions. Use your head."

The boy shrugged but trusted that the person, who had been around much longer than he had, knew what was best for him.

He opened his box and placed his
strong feelings inside it...

. . . just to be safe.

He stepped onto the other path and continued on his journey.

Here, there was less room for skipping and sidestepping. And rolling was definitely not allowed. But then, the boy spotted something beautiful.

"Flowers!"

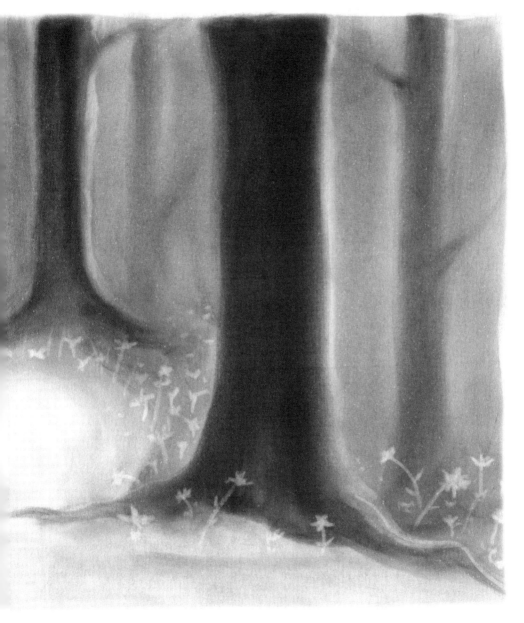

He veered off the path to pick some for his box.

"You can't stop," someone said to him.

"But I need flowers,"
the boy replied, a little irritated now.

"There's no time for that. You've got
a long journey ahead of you, and big,
important things to do,"
the person snapped.
"And besides, boys don't stop for flowers."

"I stopped for flowers,"
the boy said.
"And I'm a boy."

"And I hope you've learned from it,"
the person replied.

In truth, the boy had learned nothing.
Except that maybe some people were
really mean sometimes.

"Are you crying?"
the person said.
"Please stop."

The boy hadn't noticed the tears
trickling down his face.

He opened the box, slipped his tears in, and closed it tight, making sure everything stayed inside...

...hidden away from the world.

With every step, the boy grew
more uncertain.

And when he came to a tunnel,
he stopped.

No matter how hard he squinted,
all he saw was darkness.

"Well,"
someone said.
"What are you waiting for?"

"It's dark,"
the boy said, hoping the person might help.

"And?"

"I'm scared," the boy said.

"Boys don't get scared,"
was all the person had to say.

The boy didn't think it was that simple. But if he could put his feelings and his tears away,

maybe his fears could also go in the box.

The boy picked up his heavy load
and stepped into the tunnel.

"Good boy,"
the person said.
"I am proud of you."

The boy might have also felt proud,
but all his feelings were in his box.

Through darkness, the boy plodded on,
staying focused on the path before him.
When he stopped in front of a mountain,
he spoke before anyone else could.

"I can't climb that,"
he said.
"It's too high."

"Can't?"
someone guffawed.
"Use your arms and legs!"

"But... I don't want to,"
the boy protested.

"Such silly words. Put your box down
and climb,"
the person insisted.
"Everything you want is waiting on the
other side."

The boy was taken aback. How could this person possibly know what he wanted?

"It's what all boys want,"
the person boomed, as if he'd read
the boy's thoughts.
"Trust me. I know."

With nothing left to say, the boy put his words away.

He took one last look at his bursting box
and began to scale the mountain.

"Faster, boy!"

The boy
couldn't go
any faster
but he kept
climbing.

He gripped
and stepped
and pressed
and pulled...

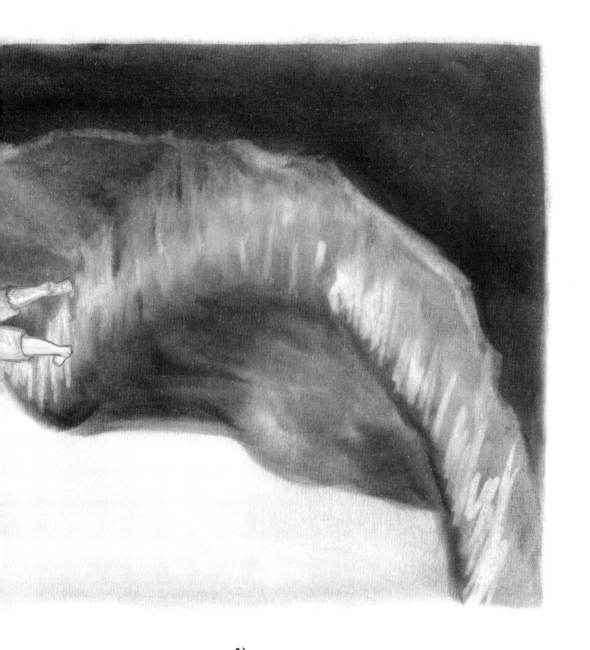

...until he
could see
the other
side.

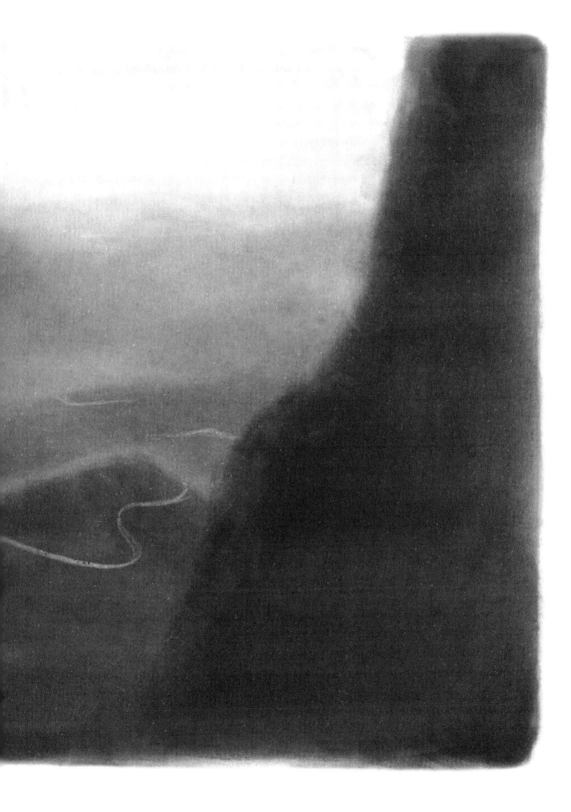

"Well done!"
the person yelled from the bottom.
"You should be happy!"

The boy was sore and weary,
but he wasn't happy.

He was…empty.

"You're much faster without your box.
Now keep going."

"My box,"
the boy whispered.

He looked down, crinkled his nose, and squinted. His box was still there. And beside it was the girl he'd met on his journey.

With one hand, she waved at him and with
the other, she held a box of her own.

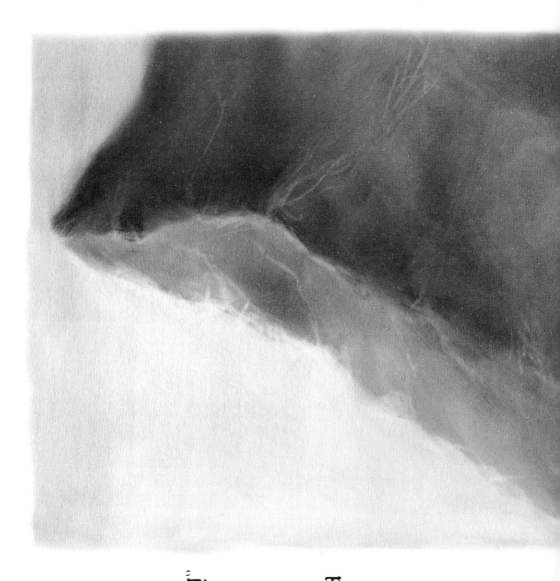

"You're going the wrong way!" the person called out.

But the boy had already begun his descent.

He sidestepped,
looped around,
and rolled
until...

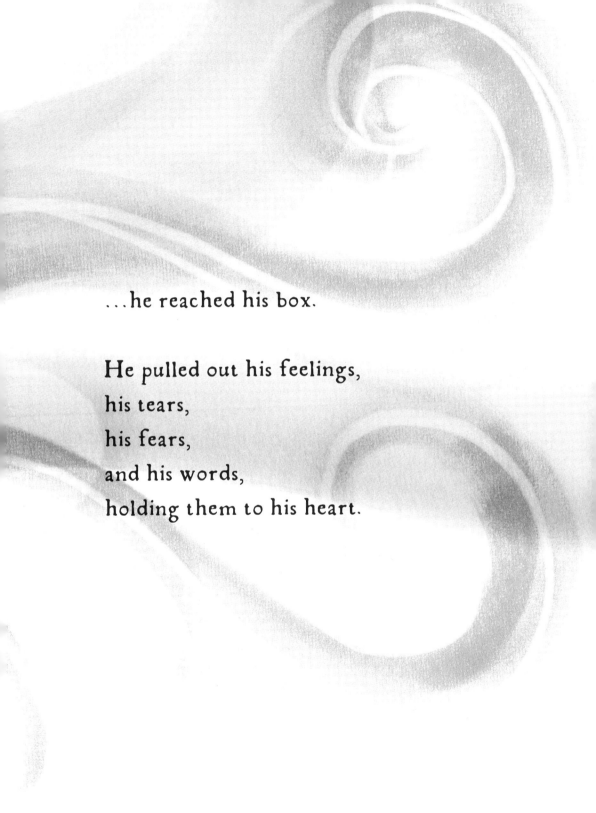

...he reached his box.

He pulled out his feelings,
his tears,
his fears,
and his words,
holding them to his heart.

"Is that a box?"
the boy asked.

"It's anything I want it to be,"
the girl said.

"That's wonderful."

With his heart full and his box empty,

the boy turned back around and skipped
down the road...

...stopping along the way for flowers.

A Note from Shameer

When I was growing up, I enjoyed watching my mum cook and I wanted a kitchen set so I could pretend to cook too. I was told, however, that it was not something a young boy should play with. So, I gave up the idea and conformed to what society expected of me. Years later, I realised that I should not have abandoned my interests just to please others. I learned the importance of listening to myself and focusing on doing what I love.

As an early childhood educator, I feel a strong sense of duty to create a safe space for the children under my care. A seven-year-old boy once confided in me. "Mr Shameer," he told me, "I don't think the boys like me because I don't like to run around like them." I looked at him and said, "Be you." And I advised him to do what he loved, be it crafts or board games, and to invite the boys to play with him, which he did. To his surprise, the boys joined him and they folded paper planes together.

To all the wonderful boys reading this — know that there is nothing braver than embracing who you are. So, give your inner self room to grow strong. When you do that, you will be unstoppable.

— Shameer Bismilla

About the Authors and Illustrator

Leila Boukarim was born in Lebanon and grew up in five different countries. Like most life journeys, Leila's has been filled with both good things and not so good things, but all of those things made her who she is today. It's taken her time, but she's learned to only take advice that will serve her and to always listen to her heart. Her path ultimately brought her to Singapore where she became a picture book author, something she hadn't planned on doing, but is so very glad she did.

Shameer Bismilla is a trained early childhood specialist. He is passionate about literacy instruction and how books can nurture the whole child. This inspired him to co-author *The Boy and the Box* and *The Girl and the Box* to create the reader's journey and challenge societal expectations. Shameer coaches and mentors teachers in literacy instruction as an adjunct lecturer at the National Institute of Early Childhood Development. He also teaches at the German European School in Singapore.

Barbara Moxham was born in Munich, raised in Sydney and calls Singapore home. She is so grateful to have grown up with parents who encouraged her creativity and confidence and taught her to be true to herself even when things are not easy. She has an incurable art and book addiction and a passion for cultivating children's emotional intelligence, all of which led to her becoming a children's book illustrator.

Text © 2020 Leila Boukarim and Shameer Bismilla
Illustrations © 2020 Barbara Moxham

Reprinted 2021

Published by Marshall Cavendish Children
An imprint of Marshall Cavendish International

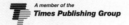

A member of the
Times Publishing Group

Other Marshall Cavendish Offices:
Marshall Cavendish Corporation, 800 Westchester Ave, Suite N-641, Rye Brook, NY 10573, USA •
Marshall Cavendish International (Thailand) Co Ltd, 253 Asoke, 16th Floor, Sukhumvit 21 Road,
Klongtoey Nua, Wattana, Bangkok 10110, Thailand • Marshall Cavendish (Malaysia) Sdn Bhd,
Times Subang, Lot 46, Subang Hi-Tech Industrial Park, Batu Tiga, 40000 Shah Alam,
Selangor Darul Ehsan, Malaysia

Marshall Cavendish is a registered trademark of Times Publishing Limited

National Library Board, Singapore Cataloguing-in-Publication Data

Name(s): Boukarim, Leila, author. | Bismilla, Shameer, author. | Moxham, Barbara, illustrator.
Title: The boy and the box / Leila Boukarim & Shameer Bismilla ; illustrated by Barbara Moxham.
Description: Singapore : Marshall Cavendish Children, [2020]
Identifier(s): OCN 1184235468 | ISBN 978-981-48-9347-3 (hardcover)
Subject(s): LCSH: Decision-making--Juvenile fiction. | Self-actualization (Psychology)--Juvenile fiction.
Classification: DDC 428.6--dc23

Printed in Singapore